TIMELESS SHAKESPEARE

OTHELLO

William Shakespeare

– ADAPTED BY –

Emily Hutchinson

SADDLEBACK
EDUCATIONAL PUBLISHING

TIMELESS SHAKESPEARE

Hamlet

Julius Caesar

King Lear

Macbeth

The Merchant of Venice

A Midsummer Night's Dream

Othello

Romeo and Juliet

The Tempest

Twelfth Night

SADDLEBACK
EDUCATIONAL PUBLISHING
www.sdlback.com

© **2003, 2011 by Saddleback Educational Publishing**

ISBN-13: 978-1-61651-108-1
ISBN-10: 1-61651-108-7
eBook: 978-1-60291-842-9

Printed in the United States of America
16 15 14 13 12   2 3 4 5 6 7

| Contents |

– INTRODUCTION –

This play is set in Venice, Italy, and the island of Cyprus in the Mediterranean Sea. The time is the early 1600s. Othello, a Moor from northwest Africa, is the great army general of Venice. As the play opens, Othello's ensign Iago has been passed over for a promotion. Instead, Othello has promoted Cassio, a younger man. Iago is very angry. To get revenge, he plans to drive a wedge between Othello and his bride, Desdemona, by playing on Othello's jealousy. As the play continues, the noble Moor falls into Iago's trap, and tragedy follows.

– CAST OF CHARACTERS –

DUKE OF VENICE

BRABANTIO Desdemona's father, a senator

GRATIANO Brabantio's brother; a noble Venetian

LODOVICO a relative of Brabantio; a noble Venetian

OTHELLO a noble Moor in the military service of Venice

CASSIO Othello's honorable lieutenant

IAGO Othello's ensign; a villain

RODERIGO an easily fooled young gentleman

MONTANO the governor of Cyprus before Othello

CLOWN Othello's servant

DESDEMONA Brabantio's daughter; Othello's fair young bride

EMILIA Iago's wife

BIANCA a prostitute

GENTLEMEN, SAILORS, OFFICERS, MESSENGER, HERALD, MUSICIANS, SERVANTS, and **SENATORS (SIGNIORS)**

ACT 1

| Scene 1 |

*(Enter **Roderigo** and **Iago** on a street in Venice.)*

RODERIGO: Why didn't you say so earlier?

IAGO: You never listen to me anyway.

RODERIGO: But you told me you hated him—

IAGO: I do. I deserve to be his lieutenant.
    Yet he picked Michael Cassio instead.
    Cassio has never proved himself in battle.
    And I, who led men on many battlefields,
    Will be Othello's mere ensign, the lowest
        rank of officer!

RODERIGO: I would rather be his hangman.

IAGO: A new system is in place.
    It's who you know that counts—not what
        you can do.
    Now, sir, judge for yourself whether I have
        any reason
    To love the Moor.

RODERIGO: Why do you follow him, then?

IAGO: Don't be fooled. I only follow him to
    get back at him.

We can't all be in charge—nor can all
    those in charge be truly followed.
In following him, I'm looking out for my
    own good.
As heaven is my judge, I act not out of
    love and duty,
Even though I must make a show of
    service.
I am never what I seem to be.

RODERIGO: We can't let him get away with this!

IAGO: Let us wake up Desdemona's father.
    Making him angry will lessen Othello's joy.

RODERIGO: Here is her father's house.

IAGO: Wake him! Yell as if the town is on fire!

RODERIGO: Hello! Brabantio! Signior
    Brabantio! Hello!

IAGO: Wake up, Brabantio! Thieves! Thieves!

BRABANTIO *(appearing above, at a window)***:** Why all
    the noise? What's wrong?

RODERIGO: Heavens, sir, you've been robbed!
    Your heart is burst. You have lost half your
    soul.
    Even now, an old black ram is mating
    with your white ewe.
    Arise! Wake your neighbors with the bell,
    Or else the devil may make you a
    grandfather.

BRABANTIO: Have you lost your mind? Who are you?

RODERIGO: I am Roderigo, sir. Don't you know my voice?

BRABANTIO: You are not welcome here!
I've told you my daughter is not for you.

RODERIGO: I have come to you with simple and pure reasons.

IAGO *(supporting Roderigo)***:** We're here to help you. If you don't act quickly, your daughter will be mated with a Moorish horse. You'll have chargers for grandsons.

BRABANTIO: What kind of foul talk is that?

IAGO: It is the truth, sir. Your daughter and the Moor are now making the beast with two backs.

BRABANTIO: Villain! You'll answer for this.

RODERIGO: Sir, I will answer anything. Maybe it is your wish
That your fair daughter, in the middle of the night,
Has been carried off in the gross embrace of a lustful Moor.
If so, we must apologize for bothering you.
But if you did not know about it, then you should thank us.

7

Why don't you find out for yourself?
  If she is in her room or your house,
Bring the justice of the state against me
  for thus lying to you.

BRABANTIO: Give me a candle! Wake up the
  household!
  Light, I say! *Light!*

(He exits from the balcony above.)

IAGO *(to Roderigo)***:** Farewell, for I must leave you.
  It wouldn't help me to be used as a
    witness against Othello.
  I know that he is in favor with the state.
  Oh, he might get some slight punishment.
  But the state needs him to lead in the
    Cyprus wars.
  Though I hate him, I must show outward
    signs of love.
  Bring the search party to the inn. I will be
    there with him. Farewell!

*(**Iago** exits. **Brabantio** enters below. **Servants**
carrying torches are with him.)*

BRABANTIO: It is too true an evil. She is gone!
  What's left of my life will be nothing but
    bitterness.
  Now, Roderigo, where did you see her?
  Oh, the foolish girl!

With the Moor, you said? Oh, treason of
the blood!
How did you know it was she? Oh, she
deceived me!
Wake up my family! Are they already
married, do you think?

RODERIGO: Truly, I think they are.

BRABANTIO: Oh, heavens! How did she get out?
Such deception!
Fathers, from now on, do not trust your
daughters' minds
Based on how you see them act. Is there
not magic
By which the nature of youth and
virginity
May be abused? Haven't you, Roderigo,
read of such things?

RODERIGO: Yes, sir, I have indeed.

BRABANTIO: Oh, if only she had been yours!
Do you know where we may find her and
the Moor?

RODERIGO: I think I can find them.

BRABANTIO: Please, lead on! Good Roderigo,
I'll reward you for this.

| Scene 2 |

*(**Othello**, **Iago**, and **servants** enter on another street.)*

IAGO: Though I have killed men in war,
It goes against my conscience to commit
murder.
I'm not evil enough to serve my own
needs. Nine or ten times
I thought about stabbing Brabantio right
here, under the ribs.

OTHELLO: It's better that you didn't.

IAGO: But he spoke rudely, insulting you.
I could hardly keep from attacking him!
But, I ask you, sir—are you married? You
can be sure of this:
Brabantio will see that you are divorced,
Or bring whatever charges against you
that the law allows.

OTHELLO: Let him do his worst.
The services that I have done for the state
Will speak louder than his complaints. No
one knows this yet,
But when the right time comes, I will
make it known that
I am descended from men of royal rank.
I can claim as great a fortune as my wife can.
Know this, Iago: If I didn't love the gentle
Desdemona so much,

I would not have given up my freedom for
   all the treasure in the sea.
But look! What lights are coming this way?

*(Enter **Cassio** and other **officers**, with **servants**
carrying torches.)*

IAGO: That's the awakened father and his
   friends! You'd better go in.

OTHELLO: No. I must be found. My talents, my
   title, and my perfect soul
Shall speak right of me. Is it they?

IAGO: I don't think so.

OTHELLO *(to Cassio's group)*: Greetings, friends!
   What is the news?

CASSIO: The duke sends greetings, General.
   And wants to see you right away.

OTHELLO: What do you think is the matter?

CASSIO: Some news from Cyprus, I imagine.
   Many important men are with the duke
     already.
They are calling for you, too.
When they did not find you at home,
The Senate sent three groups to find you.

OTHELLO: It's good that you have found me.
   I must tell my household I am leaving.
     Then I'll go with you. *(He exits.)*

CASSIO *(to Iago)*: Ensign, why is Othello here?

11

IAGO: To tell you the truth, he has boarded
    a rich vessel tonight.
  If it turns out to be a lawful prize, he'll
    be rich for life.

CASSIO: I do not understand.

IAGO: He's married.

CASSIO: To whom?

*(**Othello** re-enters.)*

IAGO: Why, to—Come, captain, ready to go?

OTHELLO: I am ready.

CASSIO: Here's another troop looking for you.

*(Enter **Brabantio**, **Roderigo**, and **officers** carrying torches and weapons.)*

IAGO: It is Brabantio! General, be warned:
  He comes with bad intentions.

OTHELLO: Hello! Stand right there!

RODERIGO *(to Brabantio)*: Signior, it is the Moor.

BRABANTIO: Down with him, the thief!

(Both groups of men draw their swords.)

OTHELLO: Put away your bright swords.
  The dew will rust them.
  (to Brabantio): Good signior, it's better
    to use the wisdom of your age
  Than weapons to make your point.

BRABANTIO: Oh, you foul thief! Where have
you hidden my daughter?
You've put a spell on her. Why else would
a girl like her—
So tender, fair, and happy—be with you?
She has refused the best men in Venice.
Surely you have cast a foul spell on her!
You must have used drugs or minerals that
weaken the will.
Therefore, I arrest and charge you as a
Practicer of forbidden and illegal arts.

OTHELLO: Where must I go to answer this
charge of yours?

BRABANTIO: To prison, until you are called to
trial by the court.

OTHELLO: I will gladly obey. But what about
the duke, who has sent these messengers
(pointing to Cassio and his men) to bring me
to him?

BRABANTIO: What? The duke is in council
At this time of the night? Let's go see him!
Mine is not a minor case.
The duke himself would feel this wrong
As if it were his own.
If, after such actions, you're allowed to go
free,
Then bond-slaves and pagans shall our
statesmen be.

| Scene 3 |

*(The **duke** and **senators** sit at a table in the council chamber.)*

DUKE *(pointing to letters on the table)*: These
    reports tell different stories.

FIRST SENATOR: Indeed, they are quite different.
    Mine says 107 ships.

DUKE: My report says 140.

SECOND SENATOR: And mine says 200!
    They don't agree about the number—
    But they all agree that a Turkish fleet is
    approaching Cyprus.

DUKE: Yes, that news does seem clear.

FIRST SENATOR: Here come Brabantio and the
    valiant Moor.

*(Enter **Brabantio, Othello, Cassio, Iago, Roderigo,** and **officers**.)*

DUKE: Valiant Othello, we must send you
    Against our enemy, the Turks.
    (to Brabantio): Oh! I did not see you.
    Welcome, gentle signior. We missed
    Your counsel and your help tonight.

BRABANTIO: And I missed yours.
    Your good grace, pardon me.
    Neither my position, nor anything I heard
    of your business

Has raised me from my bed.
Nor do public concerns take hold of me.
My particular grief is so intense it floods
   and swallows all other sorrows.

DUKE: Why? What's the matter?

BRABANTIO: My daughter! Oh, my daughter!

FIRST SENATOR: Dead?

BRABANTIO: Yes, to me!
She has been deceived, stolen from me,
   and corrupted
By spells and drugs bought from a quack.
It's against her nature to act like this—
So it must have been caused by witchcraft.

DUKE: I swear we shall punish whoever has
   done this—
Even if it is my own son.

BRABANTIO: I thank your grace humbly.
Here is the man—this Moor—the very
   man
Brought to you by your own messengers.

DUKE (to Othello)**:** What can you say to this?

OTHELLO: Most noble and honored signiors,
That I have taken this old man's daughter
   is true.
True, I have married her.
My offense is no greater than this.
I am not a gifted speaker. Yet, if I may,

I will tell the honest tale of my love and
the mighty magic
(for this is what I am charged with)
I used to win his daughter.

BRABANTIO: This maiden was never bold.
Her spirit was so quiet that she blushed at
everything.
I therefore say again that he used some
powerful drug on her.

DUKE: To swear this does not prove it.
Without some proof, you can hardly speak
against him.

OTHELLO: I ask you to send for the lady.
Let her speak of me before her father.
If her report of me is evil, take away the
honors you've given me.
Then, let your sentence fall upon my life.

DUKE: Bring Desdemona here.

(Two or three men exit.)

OTHELLO *(to Iago)***:** Ensign, lead them. You know
where she is.

*(**Iago** exits.)*

*(to the duke and senators)***:** Until she gets here,
I shall tell you
How this fair lady and I fell in love.
Her father loved me and often invited me
to his home.

He asked me for the story of my life.
I told of my dangerous travels, of terrible
  accidents in floods and on the field.
I told of being taken prisoner by enemies
And sold into slavery.
I spoke of my escape and my adventures
  in vast caves and idle deserts.
Desdemona listened carefully until
  household duties would call her away.
Whenever she could, she'd come again,
And with a greedy ear devour my story.
One day, I found a convenient time
And told her my story all at once.
Before this, she had only heard it in bits.
She often cried when I spoke of my youth.
My strange and sad story done, she said
  she wished that heaven had made such a
  man for her.
She said, if I had a friend who loved her,
I should teach him how to tell my story.
That alone would woo her.
I took her hint and spoke up for myself.
She loved me because of the dangers I had
  experienced.
I loved her because she was so moved by
  them.
This is the only witchcraft I have used.
Here comes the lady. Let her speak for
  herself.

17

*(Enter **Desdemona, Iago,** and **attendants**.)*

DUKE *(aside)*: I think this tale would win my
daughter, too!
Good Brabantio, you'll have to make the
best of it.

BRABANTIO: I beg you, hear her speak.
If she says that she was half the wooer,
May I be punished for my unjust blame of
Othello!
(to Desdemona): Come here, gentle lady.
Do you see the person to whom
You owe the most obedience?

DESDEMONA: I see here a divided duty, my
    noble father.
I owe you for my life and education,
For I am your daughter.
But here stands my husband.
As much duty as my mother showed
To you, preferring you before her father,
So I must now show to the Moor, my lord.

BRABANTIO *(to Desdemona):* God be with you!
    I'm done with it.

DUKE *(to Brabantio):* Let me say something
To help you accept these lovers.
To grieve over a misfortune that is past
Is the surest way to more misfortunes.
A robbed person who smiles
    steals something from the thief;
He robs himself who cries a pointless
    grief.
Now we must proceed to affairs of state.
The Turks are heading for Cyprus.
Othello, you are the best man to go there
    and defend it for us.

OTHELLO: I will. But my wife will need a
    proper home.

DUKE: If it please you, let it be at her father's.

BRABANTIO: I will not have it so!

OTHELLO: Nor I.

DESDEMONA: Nor I. Let me go with Othello.

OTHELLO: Let her have your permission.
  If I neglect my duties when she is with
    me,
  Let housewives make a skillet of my
    helmet
  And evil attack my good name!

DUKE: It's up to you if she stays or goes.
  The business in Cyprus is urgent.
  Othello, you must leave in one hour.
  (to Brabantio): And, noble signior, if virtue
    is a sign of beauty,
  Your son-in-law is far more fair than
    black!

BRABANTIO *(to Othello)*: Watch her, Moor.
  She has deceived her father, and may
    deceive you, too.

*(**Brabantio, duke, senators,** and **officers** exit.)*

OTHELLO: I'd stake my life on her fidelity!
  Honest Iago, I must leave my Desdemona
    to your care
  Until she is ready to follow me.
  Let your wife attend to her, and bring
    them both along when the time is best.
  Come, Desdemona. We have but an hour,
  And must obey the time.

*(**Othello** and **Desdemona** exit.)*

RODERIGO: Iago, what should I do?

IAGO: Why, go to bed and sleep.

RODERIGO: I will go and drown myself.

IAGO: How silly you are!

RODERIGO: It is foolish to live when living is torment.

IAGO: Come, be a man! Drown yourself? Drown cats and blind puppies! I am speaking as your friend. Put money in your purse. Go to the wars. Before long, Desdemona will grow tired of the Moor. Othello is too old for her. She will look for someone younger. Therefore, make all the money you can. She will soon be yours. Forget about drowning yourself. Take your chances on being hanged for trying to get what you want. A pox on drowning!

RODERIGO: Are you sure of this?

IAGO: You can count on it. Go, make money! I have told you often, and I tell you again—I hate the Moor. I hate him from the bottom of my heart. You have no less reason to hate him. Let us help each other get revenge against him. We'll talk more about this tomorrow at my lodging.

RODERIGO: I'll be there early.

IAGO: Go on, good night. No more talk of drowning, do you hear?

RODERIGO: I am changed. I'll sell all my land.

*(**Roderigo** exits.)*

IAGO: This is how I profit off a fool!
I have good reason to hate the Moor.
Gossip says that he seduced my wife.
The hint is enough to make me believe it.
Othello thinks well of me.
That will make my revenge easier.
Cassio's a handsome man with fine
    manners. Let me see now—how can I
    use that to my advantage?
Yes, I'll suggest to Othello
That Cassio is too familiar with his wife.
Men who look like Cassio are built to
    make women turn unfaithful.
The Moor is of a free and open nature.
He thinks a man is good if he seems so.
Yes, he will be easily fooled.
I have it! It is decided! Hell and night
Must bring this wicked plan to light.

(Exit.)

ACT 2

| Scene 1 |

*(**Montano** and **two gentlemen** enter a seaport in Cyprus as a storm rages.)*

MONTANO: I have never seen a worse storm.
    What do you think will happen?

SECOND GENTLEMAN: The Turkish fleet is sure to
    be destroyed.
    It will be impossible to survive this.

*(Enter a **third gentleman**.)*

THIRD GENTLEMAN: News, lads! Our wars are done!
    These angry waters have destroyed the
        Turks' ships.
    A noble ship of Venice has sighted the
        terrible wrecks and the sufferings
    Of most of the Turkish fleet. That ship
        has landed here, and
    A man from Verona has come on shore.
    He is Michael Cassio, lieutenant to the
        warlike Moor.
     The Moor himself is still at sea and on
        his way here.

MONTANO: I'm glad to hear it. Othello will be a worthy governor.

THIRD GENTLEMAN: But Cassio, though he tells good news about the Turkish loss,
Is very worried about the Moor.

MONTANO: Let us pray that he is safe.

*(Enter **Cassio**.)*

CASSIO: Thank you, valiant men of this war-torn island
Who so honor the Moor! Oh, let the heavens keep him safe!

MONTANO: Is his ship a good one?

CASSIO: His ship is strong, and his pilot has expert skills.

(Offstage, a voice cries, "A sail, a sail, a sail!")

CASSIO *(to second gentleman)*: Sir, go see who is arriving.

SECOND GENTLEMAN: I shall. *(**He** exits.)*

MONTANO: Good lieutenant, is your general married?

CASSIO: Yes. To a woman whose beauty and reputation are flawless.

*(Re-enter **second gentleman**.)*

SECOND GENTLEMAN: Iago, ensign to the general, has landed.

CASSIO: That's good. He has with him the
divine Desdemona.

MONTANO: Who is she?

CASSIO: Othello's good wife.
She was left in Iago's protection.
Now may the heavens bring Othello safely
to Desdemona's arms.

*(Enter **Desdemona, Emilia, Iago, Roderigo,** and
attendants.)*

Greetings to you, lady! May the grace of
heaven surround you.

DESDEMONA: Thank you, Cassio. What news do
you have of my husband?

CASSIO: I know only that he is well and will
soon be here.

DESDEMONA: Oh, but I'm afraid! How did your
ships get separated?

CASSIO: The storm parted us. But listen!

(Offstage a voice cries, "A sail, a sail!")

CASSIO: Go see who's coming.

*(**Second gentleman** exits.)*

(to Iago): Good ensign, you are welcome.
(to Emilia): Welcome, madam.

*(Cassio kisses the hand of Emilia. Then he kisses the
hand of Desdemona.)*

(to Iago): I hope this doesn't bother you, good Iago. It's my upbringing
That teaches me to make such a bold show of courtesy.

IAGO *(to himself)*: Good! He kisses her hand. In such a little web, I can catch a fly as big as Cassio. Yes, smile at her—go ahead! I'll catch you in your own courtesy. If your actions make you lose your position, you'll wish you hadn't been such a courtly gentleman! Very good. Well kissed! What lovely manners!

(A trumpet blows offstage.)

(to Cassio): It's the Moor! I know his trumpet.

*(Enter **Othello** and **attendants**.)*

OTHELLO: Oh, my soul's joy!

DESDEMONA: My dear Othello!

(Othello kisses Desdemona.)

IAGO *(aside)*: Oh, you are in tune with each other now!
But I'll untune the strings that make this music, as honest as I am.

OTHELLO: Come, let's go to the castle.
News, friends! Our wars are done. The Turks are drowned.
(to Desdemona): You'll be well-loved in

Cyprus, my dear—
I've found great affection here.

(Everyone but **Iago** and **Roderigo** exits.)

IAGO (to Roderigo)**:** Meet me soon at the harbor.
Be sure to come. Cassio keeps watch on
the guardhouse tonight. But first, I must
tell you this: Desdemona
is madly in love with him.

RODERIGO: With *Cassio?* Why, it isn't possible!

IAGO: Keep quiet, and just listen to me.
Remember how violently she first loved
the Moor? And just because he bragged
and told her fantastic lies? Will she keep
loving him just to hear his babbling?
Don't you believe it. She needs a man
who is closer to her own age. Nature
itself will force her to seek someone new.
Cassio is the obvious choice. He's a very
flattering rascal. Besides, he's handsome!
He has all those qualities that foolish and
young minds look for. He's a completely
rotten rascal. And the woman has fallen
for him already!

RODERIGO: I cannot believe that about her. She
has a blessed character.

IAGO: Blessed, my eye! If she was truly
blessed, she would never have loved the

Moor. Blessed, my foot! Didn't you see Cassio kissing her hand?

RODERIGO: Yes, I did. It was just courtesy.

IAGO: It was lechery, I tell you! Their lips were so close their very breaths embraced! Bah! But, sir, do as I say. Watch carefully tonight. Cassio does not know you. Find some way to make him angry. Talk too loud, or say something to offend him—whatever you can think of at the time. He is very short-tempered. Maybe he'll try to hit you. Provoke him to that, if you can. That's all I need to start a mutiny against Cassio and have him thrown out of Cyprus. That way, you'll have a quicker route to Desdemona. But first, we must remove the one obstacle that stands in front of both of us.

RODERIGO: I will do this, if it will give me any advantage.

IAGO: I guarantee it! Meet me soon at the castle. Goodbye.

RODERIGO: Goodbye. *(Exit **Roderigo**.)*

IAGO *(aside)***:** I really do believe that Cassio loves her. It is natural and likely that she loves him, too.
As much as I hate him, the Moor
Has a faithful, loving, and noble nature.

I'm sure he'll be a dear husband to her.
Now, I love her, too—but not completely
out of lust.
I love her because she'll help me get revenge,
Since I suspect the lusty Moor has seduced
my wife.
The thought of that gnaws at my insides.
Nothing will satisfy me until Othello and
I are even, wife for wife.
If I fall short of that, I'll still make him
So jealous that good sense won't cure him.
To get this done, the worthless Venetian,
Roderigo,
Must do what I've told him. Then I'll
have Michael Cassio in my pocket
(for I'm afraid that Cassio, too, has been
in my marriage bed)
And the Moor will thank me, love me,
and reward me
For making a complete fool of him!
That's the plan, though it's still a bit confused.
Evil's face is not clear until it's too late.

| Scene 2 |

*(A **herald**, with a proclamation, enters a street.)*

HERALD: It is Othello's wish that everyone
celebrate the drowning of the Turkish

fleet. Some should dance, and some make bonfires. But everyone should have fun because this is also his wedding celebration! All kitchens are open. There is free feasting from the present hour of five until the bell rings eleven. Heaven bless the island of Cyprus and our noble General Othello!

*(**All** exit.)*

| Scene 3 |

*(At the castle. Enter **Othello**, **Desdemona**, **Cassio**, and **attendants**.)*

OTHELLO: Good Cassio, you are in charge of the guard tonight.
Make sure that the celebrations do not get out of hand. Goodnight for now.
(to Desdemona): Come, my dear love.

*(Exit **Othello**, **Desdemona**, and **attendants**. Enter **Iago**.)*

CASSIO: Welcome, Iago. We must go on watch now.

IAGO: Not so soon, lieutenant. It's not ten yet! I have some wine. Let us drink to the health of black Othello.

CASSIO: I have already had too much wine. I can't overdo it with any more.

IAGO: What? This is a night of rejoicing. Some friends are waiting to join us. Go, call them in.

CASSIO: I'll do it—but I don't like the idea.

*(Exit **Cassio**.)*

IAGO *(aside)*: He must drink one more cup
On top of what he's already had tonight.
That will make him quicker to argue and
    take offense.
That lovesick fool Roderigo has already
    been toasting Desdemona tonight.
He's drained many cups to the bottom
    When he's supposed to be on guard.
Three boys of Cyprus, whom I've made
    drunk with flowing wine,
Are on guard, too. Now, among all these
    drunkards
I'll provoke Cassio to some action
That will cause offense on the island. But
    here they come!

*(Enter **Cassio, Montano**, and **gentlemen. Servants**
follow with wine.)*

CASSIO: By God, I've had a huge cup already.

MONTANO: Come now! It's just a little one, no more than a pint.

IAGO: Some wine over here!

31

(Iago sings a few drinking songs, which Cassio admires. The men continue drinking and toasting Othello's health. At last, Cassio gets ready to leave.)

CASSIO: Let us see to our business. Do not think, gentlemen, that I am drunk. *(pointing to Iago)*: This is my ensign. *(holding up each hand)*: This is my right hand, and this is my left. I am not drunk now. I can stand and speak well enough.

*(**Cassio** exits, obviously drunk.)*

MONTANO: Come, gentlemen, it's time to begin the watch.

IAGO *(pointing in Cassio's direction)*: You see him? Cassio is a soldier fit to stand beside Caesar and give orders.
But take a look at this vice of his.
It is the exact equal of his virtue—one is as strong as the other.
Because of Cassio's weakness, I fear that the trust Othello puts in him
Will one day cause trouble on this island.

MONTANO: But is he like this very often?

IAGO: Always, before he goes to bed.
He'd be awake all night if his drinking didn't put him to sleep.

MONTANO: Does the general know? It would be a good idea to tell him about this.

*(Enter **Roderigo**.)*

IAGO *(aside to Roderigo)*: What are you doing
    here, Roderigo?
  Go after the lieutenant!

*(Exit **Roderigo**.)*

MONTANO: It's a pity that the noble Moor
    Should have a weak man in such an
      important position.
  It would be wise to say so to the Moor.

IAGO: I wouldn't do it for this entire fair
    island!
  I love Cassio very much. I will try to help
    him with his problem.
  But listen! What's that noise?

*(A voice from offstage cries "Help!" Enter **Cassio**,
chasing **Roderigo**.)*

CASSIO: Damn, you villain! You rascal!

MONTANO: What's the matter, Lieutenant?

CASSIO: Do I need a villain to teach me my duty?
  I'll beat this knave to teach him his place!

RODERIGO: Beat me?

CASSIO: Still chattering? *(He strikes Roderigo.)*

MONTANO: No, Cassio! *(He grabs Cassio by the
    arm.)* Stop fighting.

CASSIO: Let go of me, sir, or I'll knock you
  over the head.

MONTANO: Come, come, you're drunk!

CASSIO: Drunk? *(Montano and Cassio fight.)*

IAGO *(aside to Roderigo)*: Away, I say! Go warn
 everyone of a mutiny.

*(**Roderigo** exits.)*

 Stop fighting, good lieutenant. For God's
 sake, gentlemen!

*(Offstage, a bell rings to wake the town. **Othello** and*
***attendants** enter.)*

OTHELLO: What's the matter here? How did
 this brawl get started?
 Have we turned into Turks? Are we doing
 to ourselves
 What heaven stopped the Turks from
 doing? Speak up. Who started this?

IAGO: I do not know. They were friends just a
 moment ago.
 Then, the next moment, their swords were
 out and pointed at each other
 In a bloody fight. I can't tell you how it
 started.

OTHELLO: Cassio, how did you get involved?

CASSIO: Please, pardon me. I cannot speak.

OTHELLO: Montano, what happened?

MONTANO: Worthy Othello, I am hurt badly. I
 was only defending myself.

OTHELLO: Now, I want to know how this fight
  started and who caused it.
  The one who is proved at fault—even if
  he were my twin brother—
  Will lose my friendship. This is
  outrageous! Iago, who started it?

IAGO: I'd rather have my tongue cut out
  Than to say anything against Michael
  Cassio.
  Still, I believe that speaking the truth shall
  not harm him.
  So here it is, General. Montano and I
  were talking here.
  Then a fellow came crying out for help.
  Cassio was following him with a drawn
  sword, trying to kill him.
  Sir, as Montano and I tried to stop Cassio,
  the other fellow ran away.
  I tried to catch up to him, but he outran
  me. I came back here quickly,
  Because I heard the clanking of swords
  and Cassio swearing loudly.
  Until tonight, I could never have said this
  about him.
  But men are only men—even the best
  men sometimes slip.
  I believe that Cassio must have received
  some sort of insult

From the man who ran away. It was
beyond his patience to let it go.

OTHELLO: Iago, it is your honesty and love that
lead you to excuse Cassio.
Cassio, I love you—but you will serve as
my officer no longer.

*(Enter **Desdemona**, with **attendants**.)*

DESDEMONA: What's the matter, dear?

OTHELLO: All's well now, sweetheart. Come
away to bed.
(to Montano): Sir, my doctor will take care
of your injuries.
(to attendants): Lead him away.

*(**Montano** exits, with **attendants**.)*

Iago, calm down any who have been
distracted by this brawl.
Come, Desdemona,
It's the story of a soldier's life
To have peaceful sleep disturbed by strife.

*(**All** but **Iago** and **Cassio** exit.)*

IAGO: Have you been hurt, Lieutenant?

CASSIO: Yes, beyond all hope of a cure.

IAGO: Oh, God forbid!

CASSIO: Reputation, reputation, reputation!
Oh, I have lost my reputation!

IAGO: Reputation is a foolish thing, often got without merit and lost without deserving. Come on, man! You can quickly recover the general's good graces. Appeal to him—he'll listen.

CASSIO: I'd rather ask him to hate me than forgive such a weak and drunken officer. Drunk? Babble? Fighting? Swearing? Oh, you invisible spirit of wine, let us call you the devil!

IAGO: Who was the man you were fighting? What had he done to you?

CASSIO: I don't know. I remember nothing clearly.

IAGO: Why, you seem well enough now. How did you recover so fast?

CASSIO: The devil of drunkenness has given way to the devil of anger. One flaw leads me to another. Oh, I hate myself!

IAGO: Don't be so hard on yourself. I wish all of this hadn't happened. But since it has, make the best of it.

CASSIO: If I ask him for my position again, he'll accuse me as a drunkard!

IAGO: I'll tell you what you should do. The general's wife has a great deal of influence over him. Ask for her help. She is so free, so kind, so good. She thinks it is wrong not to do *more* than people ask her to do. I'll bet my fortune that she will help you!

CASSIO: You give me good advice.

IAGO: I promise you, it comes to you out of sincere love and honest kindness.

CASSIO: I believe you. In the morning, I will beg for Desdemona's help.

IAGO: You're doing the right thing. Good night, now.

CASSIO: Good night, honest Iago.

(Cassio exits.)

IAGO *(aside)*: How would anyone say I'm a villain when I give such good advice?
Winning Desdemona's support
Is Cassio's only hope. But while she is pleading with the Moor,
I'll pour poison into his ear. I'll say she
Speaks only out of lust for Cassio.
The more good she tries to do for him,
The worse she'll look in the eyes of the Moor.
In this way, I will turn her virtue into wickedness.
Out of her goodness, I'll make the net to catch them all!

(Enter Roderigo.)

What is it, Roderigo?

RODERIGO: I've been thoroughly beaten
  tonight. I have nothing but experience to
  show for all my pains. My money is
  almost spent. So I'll soon have to return
  to Venice.

IAGO: How pathetic are those who have no
  patience!
  What wound ever healed but by degrees?
  Cassio may have beaten you, but you have
  ruined Cassio.
  Be patient. Go to bed now. You'll know
  more soon. Go on!

*(**Roderigo** exits.)*

  Two things must be done. My wife must
  speak to Desdemona about Cassio while
  I work on the Moor.
  I'll bring Othello in just when Cassio is
  appealing to Desdemona.
  Yes, that's the way!
  I won't spoil this plan by any delay.

*(**Iago** exits.)*

ACT 3

| Scene 1 |

*(Enter **Cassio** and **Iago** in front of the castle on Cyprus.)*

CASSIO: Iago, will you ask your wife to arrange a meeting with Desdemona?

IAGO: I'll send for Emilia now. Then I'll distract the Moor.

CASSIO: I humbly thank you. *(Exit **Iago**.)*
You are a kind and honest man.

*(Enter **Emilia**.)*

EMILIA: Good day, good lieutenant. I am sorry about what happened to you.
But all will be well soon. Desdemona has been speaking in your favor.

CASSIO: Still, I beg you to give me a chance to speak to her alone.

EMILIA: Please come in, then, sir. I will take you to her.

CASSIO: I am indebted to you for this.

*(**Emilia** and **Cassio** exit.)*

| Scene 2 |

*(Enter **Desdemona**, **Cassio**, and **Emilia** in the garden of the castle.)*

DESDEMONA: Be assured, good Cassio, that
I will do what I can for you.

CASSIO: Dear lady, I shall always be your
faithful servant.

DESDEMONA: I know that, and I thank you. You
can count on me.
If I promise something out of friendship, I
do it to the last detail.
My lord won't get any rest. I'll wear down
his patience.
In everything he does, I'll mix in talk
about your position.
So cheer up, Cassio. I would rather die
than let you down.

*(Enter **Othello** and **Iago**.)*

CASSIO: Madam, I'll leave now.

DESDEMONA: Why, stay and hear what I say.

CASSIO: Not now, madam. I am very
uncomfortable with this.

DESDEMONA: Well, do what you think best.

*(Exit **Cassio**.)*

IAGO: Ha! I don't like that.

41

OTHELLO: What did you say?

IAGO: Nothing, my lord.

OTHELLO: Wasn't that Cassio with my wife?

IAGO: Cassio, my lord? No, surely he would
not sneak away
So guilty-like when he saw you coming.

OTHELLO: I do believe it was he.

DESDEMONA: Greetings, my lord! I have been
talking to Cassio.
If I have any power to influence you,
accept his apology at once.
He truly loves you! If not, I can't judge an
honest face.
Please, give him back his position.

OTHELLO: Not now, sweet Desdemona. We'll
speak of this another time.

DESDEMONA: Please, dear, name the time! Let it
not be more than three days.
He's truly sorry for his mistake. You know,
if you asked anything of me,
I would do it for you. Why do you deny
my simple request?

OTHELLO: Please, say no more.
He can come to me when he wants to.
I will deny you nothing!
Now, I ask you to do this:
Please leave me alone for a little while.

DESDEMONA: Shall I deny you? No! Farewell, my lord.

*(Exit **Desdemona** and **Emilia**.)*

OTHELLO: Excellent wretch! The devil take my soul, but I really do love you!

IAGO: My noble lord—

OTHELLO: What is it, Iago?

IAGO: When you wooed my lady, did Cassio know of your love for her?

OTHELLO: He did, from beginning to end. Why do you ask?

IAGO: Oh, I was just wondering.

OTHELLO: Wondering about what, Iago?

IAGO: I did not think he had known her.

OTHELLO: Oh, yes. He often carried messages between us.

IAGO: Indeed?

OTHELLO: Yes, indeed! Do you see something wrong with that?
Please, tell me what's on your mind. Give me your worst thoughts.

IAGO: You ask me to tell my thoughts, good lord?
What if they are rotten and false? Who has such a pure heart

43

That unclean ideas do not sometimes
  creep in?

OTHELLO: You are hurting your friend, Iago, if
  you think he's been wronged
  And fail to tell him what you think.

IAGO: Since I may be mistaken, I'd rather
  keep my thoughts to myself.

OTHELLO: What do you mean?

IAGO: A man or a woman's good name,
  my dear lord,
  Is the most important jewel of the soul.
  Who steals my purse steals trash. It was
  something, now it's nothing.
  It was mine, now it's his. It has belonged
  to thousands of others.
  But he who takes from me my good name
  Robs me of that which does not enrich
  him, and makes me poor indeed.

OTHELLO: By heaven, I demand to know what
  you are thinking!

IAGO: Beware, my lord, of jealousy!
  It is a green-eyed monster that laughs at
  the meat it eats.
  It is better for a man to know for sure that
  his wife has been unfaithful
  Than to merely suspect it. How time
  drags on for the man

Who adores, but doubts; suspects, yet
  loves deeply!

OTHELLO: Why do you say this? You can't make
  me jealous
By saying my wife is lovely, eats well,
  loves company,
Speaks freely, sings, and dances well.
  In a virtuous person, these are but
  more virtues.
Though I am not perfect, I will not doubt
  her love. She had eyes, and she chose
  me. No, Iago,
I must see evidence before I doubt. And
  when I doubt, I must have proof.
When there's proof, that's the end of it.
No more love or jealousy!

IAGO: I'm glad to hear this. I have no proof, but
Watch your wife! Observe her well when
  she is with Cassio.
Remember that she deceived her father by
  marrying you.
He thought it was witchcraft—but I
  should say no more.
I beg your pardon for being too concerned
  about you.

OTHELLO: I am grateful for your concern.

IAGO: I hope you realize that I spoke only out
  of love.

But I see that you're disturbed.
I beg you not to jump to conclusions.
Suspecting something does not make it
  true.

OTHELLO: I do not think that Desdemona is
  anything but honest.

IAGO: And long may she live so! And long
  may you live to think so!

OTHELLO: And yet—

IAGO: Yes, there's one other point.
  All things in nature tend to mate
  With those who are like themselves.
  But she did not.
  One might smell in that kind of desire
    unnatural thoughts.
  But forgive me—I'm not exactly talking
    about her.
  Although I do fear that her better
    judgment might cause her to
  Compare you with men of her own race
    and later reject you.

OTHELLO: Farewell, farewell! If you see
  anything else, let me know.
  Tell your wife to observe, too. Now, I
    want to be alone, Iago.

IAGO: My lord, I'll take my leave. *(Iago starts to
  walk away.)*

OTHELLO *(to himself)*: Why did I marry?
Iago, this honest man, no doubt sees and
Knows more—much more—than he says.

IAGO *(returning)*: My lord, give this time.
Nothing is proven yet.
But keep an eye on Cassio.
Watch if your lady pleads in his favor
Too strongly or too often.
Much will be seen in that.
Meanwhile, just think of my fears as
  foolish and consider her innocent.

OTHELLO: Don't worry about me.

IAGO: Once again, I take my leave.

*(Exit **Iago**.)*

OTHELLO: This fellow is exceedingly honest.
He knows all types of people.
If he is right about Desdemona, I'll send
  her packing.
Perhaps, because I am black, or because I
  am older than she is,
She has betrayed me.
Oh, what a curse marriage is,
That we can call these delicate creatures
  ours and not control them!
I'd rather be a toad living in a dungeon
Than have a part of something I love used
  by others. Oh! Here comes Desdemona.

*(Re-enter **Desdemona** and **Emilia**.)*

> If she is false, then heaven mocks itself!
> I won't believe it.

DESDEMONA: How are you, my dear Othello?

OTHELLO: I have a pain in my forehead, here.

DESDEMONA: Why, that must be because you
haven't had enough sleep.
Let me tie my handkerchief around your
head. That will help.

OTHELLO: Your handkerchief is too little. *(He
pushes it away, and it drops to the floor.)*
Let it alone. Come, I'll go in with you.

DESDEMONA: I am sorry that you are not well.

*(Exit **Othello** and **Desdemona**.)*

EMILIA *(picking up the handkerchief)*: I am glad to
have found this.
This was her first gift from the Moor.
Iago has asked me 100 times to steal it.
But she loves it so much she always carries it,
Since Othello made her promise to always
keep it.
What Iago wants with it, heaven knows;
I don't.
I want only to please him. *(Re-enter **Iago**.)*

IAGO: Hello! What are you doing here alone?

EMILIA: I have something for you—that
handkerchief you wanted.

IAGO: Have you stolen it from her?

EMILIA: Of course not. It was dropped by accident, and I picked it up.

IAGO: Good woman! Give it to me.

EMILIA: What will you do with it?

IAGO *(grabbing it):* Why, what is it to you?

EMILIA: If it's not for something important, give it back to me.
The poor lady will go crazy when she realizes she's lost it.

IAGO: Don't let on that you know anything. I have use for it. Go, leave me.

*(Exit **Emilia**.)*

I'll put this handkerchief in Cassio's room
and let him find it.
Little things like this are quite convincing
to the jealous mind.
The Moor is already influenced by my
poisonous words.
Dangerous ideas are poisonous in their
nature.
At first they do not taste too bad, but
soon they get into the blood
And burn like sulfur.

*(Re-enter **Othello**.)*

Greetings, my lord!

OTHELLO: Unfaithful! What did I know of her
stolen hours of lust?
I didn't see it, didn't think of it, and
wasn't harmed by it.
I slept well, ate well, and was free and
merry.
I didn't know that the villain Cassio had
been kissing her.
I'd have been happy if the whole army had
made love to her—as long as I didn't
know.
Now I must say farewell to peace of mind!
Farewell to happiness!

IAGO: Is it possible, my lord?

OTHELLO: You'd better be sure of it, Iago.
Give me visible proof!
Or, by my eternal soul, you'd be better
off to be born a dog
Than to answer my awakened wrath!

IAGO: Oh, God! Oh, heaven forgive me!
Oh, monstrous world!
Take note, take note, world: To be direct
and honest is not safe.
I thank you for teaching me this lesson.
From now on,
I'll love no friend, since love causes such
offense.

OTHELLO: No, stay. You should be honest.
By all the world, I believe my wife to be
honest, and believe she is not.
I think that you are truthful, and think
that you are not.
I must have some *proof.* Her name, which
was as clean
As Diana's face, is now grimy and black as
my own face.
I wish I could be certain!

IAGO: I see, sir, you are eaten up with passion.
I am sorry that I caused this.
Do you want to be sure?

OTHELLO: Want to be? No, I *will* be!

IAGO: But how?

51

How will you be certain, my lord?
Do you want to see her in the act?

OTHELLO: Death and damnation! Oh!

IAGO: It would be very difficult to catch
them. How then?

OTHELLO: Give me absolute proof she's been
unfaithful. I'll tear her to pieces!

IAGO: I do not like being in this position.
But I'll tell you this:
I heard Cassio talking in his sleep.
He said, "Sweet Desdemona,
Let us be careful. Let us hide our love!"
Then he said, "Curse the fate that gave
you to the Moor!"

OTHELLO: Oh, monstrous! *Monstrous!*

IAGO: Still, this was just his dream.

OTHELLO: It's very suspicious, even though it
was only a dream.

IAGO: It might help to support other evidence.
Tell me, have you not sometimes seen a
handkerchief
Decorated with strawberries in your wife's
hand?

OTHELLO: Why? I gave her one like that.
It was my first gift to her.

IAGO: I didn't know that.
But I saw Cassio wipe his beard

With such a handkerchief today.

OTHELLO: If it's the same one—

IAGO: If it's the same one, or any one that is hers,
It speaks against her, along with the other
proofs.

OTHELLO: Oh, I wish she had 40,000 lives!
One is too little, too small for my revenge!
Now I see that it is true.
All my dear love for her is gone.
Now you must help me.
Within three days, let me hear you say
That Cassio is no longer alive.

IAGO: He is as good as dead, by your request.
But let her live.

OTHELLO: Damn her, the wicked minx!
Oh, damn her! I must think of
Some swift means of death for the fair devil.
You are my lieutenant now.

IAGO: I am your servant forever.

*(**Othello** and **Iago** exit.)*

| Scene 3 |

*(Enter **Desdemona** and **Emilia** in front of the castle.)*

DESDEMONA: Where could I have lost the
handkerchief, Emilia?

I would rather have lost my purse full of
    gold coins!
If my noble Moor were not so sensible,
    this would be enough
To put evil thoughts in his head.

EMILIA: Isn't he jealous?

DESDEMONA: Who, Othello? Not in the least!

EMILIA: Look, here he comes.

*(Enter **Othello**.)*

DESDEMONA *(to Othello)*: How are you, my lord?

OTHELLO: Well, my good lady.
    (to himself): Oh, it is so hard to lie!
    (to her): How are you, Desdemona?

DESDEMONA: Well, my lord. I have sent for
    Cassio to come speak with you.

OTHELLO: I have a terrible head cold. Lend me
    your handkerchief.

DESDEMONA: Here, my lord.

OTHELLO: I mean the one I gave you.

DESDEMONA: I don't have it with me.

OTHELLO: Is it lost? Is it gone? Tell me, have
    you left it somewhere?

DESDEMONA: It is not lost. But what if it were?

OTHELLO: Go get it. Let me see it.

DESDEMONA: Well, I could do that, sir, but I
    won't right now.

Now, I want to talk about Cassio.
Please give him his job back.

OTHELLO: Get me the handkerchief!

DESDEMONA: Come, come! You'll never find a
more capable man.

OTHELLO: The handkerchief!

DESDEMONA: Please, let's talk about Cassio.

OTHELLO: The *handkerchief*!

DESDEMONA: Really, you have no reason to act
this way.

OTHELLO: Get away from me! *(Exit **Othello**.)*

EMILIA: And you say he isn't jealous?

DESDEMONA: I never saw him like this before!

EMILIA: Sometimes it takes years to see what a
man is really like.

*(Enter **Cassio** and **Iago**.)*

Look, Cassio and my husband!

DESDEMONA: Cassio! What news have you?

CASSIO: Madam, the same as before.
I beg you to speak to your husband.

DESDEMONA: Oh, gentle Cassio! My words
won't help right now.
My lord is not himself. Be patient. I'll do
what I can.

IAGO: Is my lord angry?

EMILIA: Yes, for some reason he seemed strangely disturbed. He left just now.

IAGO: How can he be angry? It must be something very serious.
I'll go see about it.

*(Exit **Iago**.)*

DESDEMONA *(calling after Iago)***:** Please do.
*(to Emilia)***:** Some business of state must be bothering him.
I thought he was angry with me.
Now I realize it was something else.

EMILIA: Pray that state business concerns him rather than jealous thoughts.

DESDEMONA: I have never given him cause!

EMILIA: But jealous souls will not be answered that way.
They are never jealous for good reason, but only because they're jealous.
It is a monster that creates more of itself and was born of itself.

DESDEMONA: May heaven keep that monster from Othello's mind!

EMILIA: Amen to that, lady.

DESDEMONA: I'll look for him. Come, Emilia.

*(Exit **Desdemona** and **Emilia**. Enter **Bianca**.)*

BIANCA: Greetings, my friend Cassio.
Why haven't you been to see me?

CASSIO: I was just coming to your house.
Sweet Bianca, *(giving her Desdemona's handkerchief)* will you copy this
embroidery for me?

BIANCA: Oh, Cassio, where did you get this?
Is it a gift from a new friend?
Now I know why you haven't been to
see me lately. Well, well.

CASSIO: Go on, fair maid!
This isn't from another woman.

BIANCA: Well, whose is it?

CASSIO: I don't know, sweet. It was in my
bedroom. I like the embroidery.
Before it is reclaimed, and I'm sure it
will be, I'd like to have it copied.
Take it, and do it, and leave me alone
awhile.

BIANCA: Leave you alone? Why?

CASSIO: I'm waiting for the general. I will
see you soon.

BIANCA: All right. I'll look forward to it.

*(Exit **Cassio** and **Bianca**.)*

ACT 4

| Scene 1 |

*(Cyprus, in front of the castle: Enter **Othello** and **Iago**.)*

IAGO: Do you think so?

OTHELLO: *Think* so, Iago?

IAGO: What, to kiss in private?

OTHELLO: An unauthorized kiss.

IAGO: Or to be naked with her friend in bed
An hour or more, not meaning any harm?

OTHELLO: Naked in bed, and not mean harm?
People who act that way will be tempted
By the devil, and they will tempt heaven.

IAGO: If they do nothing, it's a forgivable sin.
But if I give my wife a handkerchief—

OTHELLO: What then?

IAGO: Why, then, it's hers, my lord. As hers,
She may, I think, give it to any man.

OTHELLO: Her honor belongs to her, too.
May she give that away?

IAGO: Her honor is a quality that's not seen.
Some seem to have it when they don't.
But, as for the handkerchief—

OTHELLO: I wish I had forgotten it!
But now I remember that he had it.

IAGO: Yes, what of it?

OTHELLO: That's not so good.

IAGO: What if I said I saw him do you wrong?
Or if I had heard him blab—

OTHELLO: What has he said?

IAGO: Why, that he did—I don't know—lie—

OTHELLO: With her?

IAGO: With her, on her—what you will.

OTHELLO: Lie with her? Lie on her? By God, that's
disgusting! Is this possible? Oh, devil!

(He falls into a trance.)

IAGO *(aside)*: My medicine is working!
This is how gullible fools are caught,
And how many worthy and chaste women,
All innocent, wind up accused.

*(Enter **Cassio**.)*

CASSIO: What happened?

IAGO: My lord has had an epileptic seizure.
Look, he's stirring now.
Step out of the way for a while.
When he recovers and leaves,
I need to talk to you. It's very important.

*(Exit **Cassio**.)*

IAGO *(to Othello)***:** How are you, General?

OTHELLO: Not well. Did he confess it?

IAGO: Good sir, take it like a man.
You're not the first man it's happened to.
Better to know the truth, don't you think?

OTHELLO: Oh, you are wise! That's certain.

IAGO: Step aside for a while.
While you were out, Cassio came by.
I made him leave, but he promised to
return later.
Why don't you hide yourself,
And observe with your own eyes
The sneers and the scorn on his face?
I will make him tell the story again
Of where, how often, and when
He has—and will again—meet your wife.
I tell you, just watch how he acts.

OTHELLO: Thank you, Iago. *(Othello hides.)*

IAGO *(to himself)***:** I'll ask Cassio about Bianca.
She's a hussy who sells herself to him
To buy herself bread and clothes.
She loves Cassio. It's typical of whores
To attract many men, but love only one.
When a man hears of her love,
He can't help but laugh. Here is Cassio.

*(Enter **Cassio**.)*

When he smiles, Othello shall go mad.

(to Cassio): How are you, Lieutenant?

CASSIO: All the worse since you call me by that title, the lack of which is killing me.

IAGO: Work on Desdemona, and you're sure to get it back.
(speaking lower): Now, if Bianca had anything to do with it,
How quickly you'd have your job back!

CASSIO: Yes, that poor fool loves me!

OTHELLO: Look how he laughs already!

IAGO: I never knew a woman so in love!

CASSIO: The pitiful wretch!

IAGO: Haven't you heard? She's saying
That you're going to marry her.
Do you really intend to?

CASSIO: Ha, ha, ha! Marry her—a prostitute?
Please give me more credit than that!
Ha, ha, ha!
She was just here. She follows me around.
I must get rid of her.

IAGO *(in a low voice)*: Well, look! Here she is.

*(Enter **Bianca**.)*

CASSIO *(to Bianca)*: Are you following me?

BIANCA: Let the devil and his mother follow you! What did you mean by giving me that handkerchief? I was a fine fool to take it! You say you found it in your bedroom and don't know who left it there? Some hussy, no doubt. Here! Give it back to your whore. I'm not copying the embroidery.

CASSIO: What's this, my sweet Bianca?

OTHELLO: By heaven, that's my handkerchief!

BIANCA: If you want to come to supper tonight, you may. If you don't, only come back again when you're invited.

*(Exit **Bianca**.)*

CASSIO: I'd better go after her. Otherwise, she'll be yelling in the streets about me.

IAGO: Will you have supper there?

CASSIO: Yes, I intend to.

IAGO: Well, I might see you later. I really need to speak with you.

CASSIO: I'll see you later, then.

*(Exit **Cassio**.)*

OTHELLO *(coming forward)*: I'll kill him, Iago!

IAGO: Did you see how he laughed at his sin? And did you see the handkerchief?

OTHELLO: I could spend nine years killing him. A fine woman! A lovely woman!

IAGO: No, you must forget all that.

OTHELLO: Yes, let her rot and perish and be damned tonight, for she shall not live! No, my heart is turned to stone. Oh, but that sweet creature could sing the savageness right out of a bear! She has such a gentle way about her!

IAGO: Yes, too gentle.

OTHELLO: That's certain now. But yet the pity of it, Iago! Oh, Iago, the pity of it!

IAGO: If you care about her that much, Why don't you just look the other way? If it doesn't bother you, it won't bother anyone.

OTHELLO: I will chop her into little bits! She made a fool of me—with my officer!

IAGO: That's even worse.

OTHELLO: Get me some poison, Iago. Tonight!

IAGO: Don't use poison. Strangle her in her bed, the very bed she has contaminated.

OTHELLO: Good, good! The justice of that pleases me. Very good!

IAGO: As for Cassio, let me take care of him. You shall hear more by midnight.

*(A trumpet blows offstage. Enter **Lodovico**, **Desdemona**, and **attendants**.)*

OTHELLO: What was that trumpet?

IAGO: Surely someone from Venice. It's Lodovico. He's come from the duke. Look, your wife is with him.

LODOVICO: The duke and senators of Venice greet you. *(He gives Othello a letter.)*

OTHELLO: I kiss this letter. *(He opens the letter and reads it.)*

LODOVICO: How's Lieutenant Cassio doing?

IAGO: He lives, sir.

DESDEMONA: Cousin, he and my lord have had A falling out. But you will make all well.

OTHELLO: Are you sure of that?

DESDEMONA: My lord?

OTHELLO *(reading)*: "Do it as soon as you can—"

LODOVICO: He wasn't speaking to you. He's
busy with his letter.
Is there trouble between my lord and Cassio?

DESDEMONA: Very bad trouble. I want them
To make up, for the love I feel for Cassio.

OTHELLO: Fire and brimstone!

DESDEMONA: My lord?

LODOVICO: Maybe the letter has upset him.
I think they want him to go home
And leave his position here to Cassio.

DESDEMONA: Well, really, I'm glad to hear it.

OTHELLO *(striking her)*: *Devil!*

DESDEMONA *(shocked and horrified)*: I've done
nothing to deserve this.

LODOVICO: My lord, no one would believe this
in Venice, even if I swore I saw it.
Apologize to her. She's weeping.

OTHELLO: Oh, devil, devil!
If the earth were sown by woman's tears,
Her tears would become crocodiles!
Out of my sight!

DESDEMONA: I will not stay to offend you.

(Weak with shock, she turns to go.)

OTHELLO: Go away! I'll send for you soon.

*(Exit **Desdemona**, crying bitterly.)*

> *(to Lodovico, furiously)*: Sir, I'll obey this
> letter and return to Venice.
> Cassio shall have my place! And, sir,
> Tonight I hope we can dine together.
> You are welcome to Cyprus.

(He bows, then leaves in a trembling rage.)

> Goats and monkeys!

LODOVICO: Is this the noble Moor whom our
senate thought to be so capable?
The man whom anger could not shake?

IAGO: He is much changed.

LODOVICO: Is his mind all right? Is he mad?

IAGO: He's what he seems to be. I wish
He could be what he might have been!

LODOVICO: And he struck his wife?

IAGO: Alas! That was not so good.
And I'm afraid he might do worse.

LODOVICO: Is he usually like this?
Or did the letter make him angry?

IAGO: Alas, alas! I should not speak about
What I have seen. Watch him yourself.

LODOVICO: I'm sorry I was wrong about him.

*(**All** exit.)*

| Scene 2 |

*(A room in the castle. Enter **Othello** and **Emilia**.)*

OTHELLO: You have seen nothing, then?

EMILIA: Nor ever heard or suspected anything.

OTHELLO: But you have seen her with Cassio?

EMILIA: Yes, but I saw no harm in it.
I heard everything they said to each other.

OTHELLO: What—they didn't even whisper?

EMILIA: Never, my lord.

OTHELLO: Nor send you out of the way?

EMILIA: Never!

OTHELLO: That's strange.

EMILIA: My lord, I would bet my soul that she
is faithful.
Never think otherwise!
If some villain has given you this idea,
Let heaven punish him.
If she isn't faithful, chaste, and true,
There's not a happy man in the world.

OTHELLO: Tell her to come to me. Go.

*(Exit **Emilia**.)*

Her words sound good. Yet any stupid
Woman could make up such a story.

*(Enter **Desdemona** and **Emilia**.)*

DESDEMONA: My lord, what do you wish?

67

OTHELLO: Let me see your eyes. Look at me.

DESDEMONA: What horrible ideas do you have?

OTHELLO *(to Emilia)*: Leave us alone and shut the
   door.

*(Exit **Emilia**.)*

OTHELLO: Tell me, what are you?

DESDEMONA: Your wife, my lord.
   Your true and loyal wife.

OTHELLO: Come, swear you are honest.

DESDEMONA: Heaven truly knows I am!

OTHELLO: Heaven knows you are false as hell.

DESDEMONA: What? To whom, my lord?
   With whom? How am I false?

OTHELLO: Ah, Desdemona! Get away! Away!

DESDEMONA: Oh, what a sad day!
   Why do you weep?
   Am I the cause of these tears, my lord?
   Do you suspect my father for having you
      called back to Venice?
   Don't blame me for it.

OTHELLO: If heaven had sent me some illness,
   Or buried me in poverty up to my lips,
   Or made me a slave, I could have taken it.
   But to be driven from the place
   Where I have gathered up my heart—
   This makes me grim as hell!

DESDEMONA: My noble lord,
  I pray you know that I am faithful.

OTHELLO: I wish you'd never been born!

DESDEMONA: Alas! What sin have I
  unknowingly committed?

OTHELLO: What sin have you committed?
  You impudent harlot!

DESDEMONA: By God, you do me wrong.

OTHELLO: Are you not a harlot?

DESDEMONA: No, I swear to you as a Christian!

OTHELLO: What—you're not a whore?

DESDEMONA: No! I swear it by heaven.

OTHELLO: Is it possible?

DESDEMONA: Oh, heaven help us!

OTHELLO: I ask your pardon, then.
  I thought you were that sly whore of
    Venice who married Othello.
  (shouting): Come here, woman!

*(Enter **Emilia**.)*

  You who have the opposite job of St. Peter
  And keep the gate of hell! You, yes, *you!*
  (giving her money): We are finished. Here's
    money for your trouble.
  Please, keep this meeting secret.

*(Exit **Othello**.)*

EMILIA: My God, what is he thinking?
  Are you all right, my good lady?

DESDEMONA: Really, I'm in shock.
  I cannot weep, and I can't say anything
  That shouldn't be said with tears.
  Make up my bed with my wedding sheets.
  And call your husband here.

EMILIA: Things are certainly changed!

*(Exit **Emilia**.)*

DESDEMONA: Heaven pity me! What have I
  done to make him think me unfaithful?

*(Enter **Iago** and **Emilia**.)*

IAGO: What can I do for you, madam?

DESDEMONA: I don't know exactly.

IAGO: What's the matter, lady?

EMILIA: Alas, Iago, my lord has cruelly called
  her a whore.

IAGO: Why did he do this?

DESDEMONA: I don't know.

IAGO: Do not weep! What a sad day!

EMILIA: Has she refused so many noble matches,
  Her father, her country, and her friends,
  To be called a whore?
  Doesn't she have a right to weep?

IAGO: Curse him for it! Why did he say this?

DESDEMONA: Only heaven knows.

EMILIA: Some villain, some cheating scoundrel
Must have told this lie to get ahead.
You can hang me if I'm wrong.

IAGO: There is no such man. It's impossible.

DESDEMONA: If there is, heaven forgive him!

EMILIA: May a noose forgive him!
And may hell gnaw on his bones!
Why should anyone call her a whore?
The Moor has been misled by a villain.

IAGO: Watch what you say.

EMILIA: Oh, to hell with him!
It was just that kind of man who
Made you think *I* was the Moor's lover!

IAGO: You are a fool. Watch yourself.

DESDEMONA: Iago, good friend, talk to him.
I tell you, I love him dearly.
His unkindness may destroy my life,
But it will never change my love.

IAGO: Don't be upset. It's just his mood.
Business of state has made him angry,
And he takes it out on you.
That's all it is, I assure you.

(Trumpets blow offstage.)

Listen, the trumpets call you to supper!
Go in, and stop crying. All will be fine.

*(Exit **Desdemona** and **Emilia**. Enter **Roderigo**.)*

Greetings, Roderigo!

RODERIGO: You've been cheating me, sir.

IAGO: In what way?

RODERIGO: You keep putting me off, Iago. I have wasted all my money. The jewels I've given you to give to Desdemona would have half-corrupted a nun. You've said that she's received them. You've led me to have hopes of getting closer to her. But it hasn't happened.

IAGO: Well, calm down. All is well.

RODERIGO: No, all is *not* well! In fact, I'm starting to feel you can't be trusted. I will make myself known to Desdemona. If she will return my jewels to me, I will leave her alone. If not, be certain that I'll make you pay.

IAGO: Well, now I see you've got some backbone. You have good cause for your anger! Still, I assure you, I have been very fair with you.

RODERIGO: It doesn't appear that way.

IAGO: I admit that. Your suspicions are not foolish. But Roderigo, I'm convinced more than ever that you have determination, courage, and valor.

Show it tonight! If Desdemona isn't yours tomorrow night, take me from this world with treachery!

RODERIGO: Well, what is your plan? Is it reasonable and possible?

IAGO: Sir, an official order came from Venice. Cassio is to take Othello's place.

RODERIGO: Is that true? Why, then, Othello and Desdemona will return to Venice.

IAGO: Oh, no. He'll go to Mauritania, taking Desdemona, unless some accident forces him to stay here. Getting rid of Cassio would simply be the accident to force that result.

RODERIGO: Getting rid of him? What do you mean?

IAGO: Why, by making him unable to take Othello's place—by knocking out his brains.

RODERIGO: That's what you want me to do?

IAGO: Yes—if you dare do the best thing for yourself. Cassio is eating with a harlot tonight. I'm going to meet him there. He doesn't know the news of his good fortune yet. If you watch for him to leave, you can finish him off at your leisure. I'll be nearby to back you up.

Between the two of us, he'll die. Don't look
so shocked, but come with me.

RODERIGO: I want to hear more reasons for this.

IAGO: You'll hear them!

*(**Roderigo** and **Iago** exit.)*

| Scene 3 |

*(Another room in the castle: Enter **Othello**, **Lodovico**, **Desdemona**, **Emilia**, and **attendants**.)*

OTHELLO *(to Lodovico)*: Walk with me, sir?
(to Desdemona): Go to bed at once. I'll
return soon. Send your servant away
now. Be sure to do it.

DESDEMONA: I will, my lord.

*(Exit **Othello**, **Lodovico**, and **attendants**.)*

EMILIA: He seems to be in a better mood.

DESDEMONA: He says he'll be back soon.
He told me to go to bed
And to send you away.

EMILIA: What? Send me away?

DESDEMONA: That was his wish. So, Emilia,
Give me my night clothes, and goodbye.
We must not displease him now.

EMILIA: I wish you had never met him!

DESDEMONA: But I don't. I love him truly.

EMILIA *(helping her change for bed)***:** I've put those
sheets you asked for on the bed.

DESDEMONA: It doesn't matter. My goodness,
how foolish we are!
If I die before you, please wrap me
In one of these same sheets.

EMILIA: Come now! What kind of talk is that?

DESDEMONA: Oh, these men! These men!
Do you honestly think—tell me, Emilia—
That there are women who are unfaithful
To their husbands?

EMILIA: There are some. No question about it.

DESDEMONA: Would you do such a deed for all
the world?

EMILIA: Why—wouldn't you?

DESDEMONA: No, I swear by the light of all the
stars that I wouldn't!

EMILIA: Well, I wouldn't do it by the light of
the stars.
It would be easier to do in the dark.

DESDEMONA: Would you truly do such a deed
for all the world?

EMILIA: The world's a huge thing.
It would be a great payment
For a small sin.

DESDEMONA: Surely you don't mean that!

EMILIA: I do. I'd make up for it once it was done. Of course, I wouldn't do such a thing for a little ring, or for property, nor for dresses, gowns, or caps, or any small gift. But for the whole world? For God's sake! Who wouldn't be unfaithful to her husband to make him a king?

DESDEMONA: Curse me if I would do such a wrong Even for the whole world!

EMILIA: Why, that wrong is just one of many in the world! And if you'd get the whole world for your trouble, then it's wrong in your own world. You could quickly make everything right again.

DESDEMONA: I do not think there is any such woman!

EMILIA: There are enough to fill the world! But I do think it is their husbands' faults When wives do wrong. Suppose they Give our valuables to other women, Or else have a fit of foolish jealousy And keep us from coming and going. Or suppose they strike us— Why, we can become resentful, too! We can even become vengeful. Wives have feelings just like husbands.

They see, smell, and have tastes
For both sweet and sour things
Just as their husbands do. Why do they
Reject us for other women? Is it for sport?
I think it is. And does it result from
    desire?
I think so. Does frailty lead them to sin?
It certainly does. And don't we have
    longings, desires, and frailty, just as
    our men do?
Let them treat us well—or let them know
We will behave just as they do, just so.

DESDEMONA: Good night, good night.
May heaven teach me
Not to return evil with evil, but to learn
    from it!

*(Exit **Desdemona** and **Emilia**.)*

ACT 5

| Scene 1 |

*(A street in Cyprus: Enter **Iago** and **Roderigo**.)*

IAGO: He'll be coming by soon, Roderigo.
  Keep your sword out. Be ready to use it.
  Quick, quick! Fear nothing. I'll be near.

RODERIGO: Stay close. I might make a mistake.

IAGO: I am right here. Be bold!

*(**Iago** hides himself.)*

RODERIGO: I'm not sure about this.
  But he has given me good reasons for it.
  It will be just another man dead.
  My sword is ready! He'll die!

IAGO *(aside)*: Very good. I've rubbed this
   young pimple almost raw,
  And now he's getting angry.
  Whether he kills Cassio, or Cassio him,
  Or they kill each other, it will all
  Be good for me. If Roderigo lives,
  He'll want me to give back all the
  Gold and jewels that I swindled from him
  As gifts for Desdemona.
  That must not happen. If Cassio survives,

The Moor might reveal my lies to him.
That would be very dangerous for me—
So he must die! I hear him coming.

*(Enter **Cassio**.)*

RODERIGO: I know his walk. It's Cassio!
Villain, prepare to die!

(Roderigo attacks Cassio with a sword, but does no damage. Cassio draws his own sword and wounds Roderigo seriously.)

RODERIGO: Oh, I've been killed!

*(**Iago** wounds Cassio's leg and quickly exits.)*

CASSIO: I've been maimed! Help! Murder! Murder! *(He falls.)*

*(Enter **Othello**.)*

OTHELLO *(to himself)***:** That's Cassio!
Iago kept his word. Oh, brave Iago!
How strongly he feels for a friend who's been wronged.
He teaches me! So now, hussy, your lover lies dead,
And your own death is near. I'm coming, harlot.
Your charms are blotted out of my heart,
And your lust-stained bed shall soon be stained with your lustful blood.

*(Exit **Othello**. Enter **Lodovico** and **Gratiano**.)*

CASSIO: Help! No passers-by? Murder!

GRATIANO: What a frightening cry!

CASSIO: Oh, help!

LODOVICO: Listen! It's so dark, I can't see.

RODERIGO: Oh, wretched villain! Won't anybody help? Then I shall bleed to death.

*(Enter **Iago**, carrying a light.)*

IAGO: Did I hear a cry?

CASSIO: Here, here! For heaven's sake, help!

IAGO: What's the matter?

CASSIO: Iago? Over here! I have been injured by villains!

IAGO: Oh, no, Lieutenant! Who has done this?

CASSIO: I think one of them is nearby And cannot get away.

IAGO: Oh, the treacherous villains! *(to Lodovico and Gratiano):* Who's over there? Come and give me some help.

RODERIGO: Oh, help me here!

CASSIO: That's one of them.

IAGO *(to Roderigo)*: You murderous scum! You villain! *(Iago stabs Roderigo.)*

RODERIGO: Oh, damned Iago! You inhuman dog! *(Roderigo dies.)*

IAGO: The idea of killing men in the dark!
Where are these bloodthirsty thieves?
This town is so silent! Ho! Murder!
Murder! *(to Lodovico and Gratiano):* Who are
you? Are you good or evil?

LODOVICO: Judge us by our actions.

IAGO: Signior Lodovico?

LODOVICO: Yes, sir.

IAGO: I beg your pardon. Here's Cassio, who's
been attacked by villains.

GRATIANO: Cassio!

IAGO: How are you, brother?

CASSIO: My leg has been cut deeply.

IAGO: I'll bandage it with my shirt.

*(Enter **Bianca**.)*

BIANCA *(seeing Cassio):* Oh, Cassio!
My dear Cassio! Oh, Cassio, Cassio!

IAGO: Gentlemen all, I suspect this slut
Had something to do with this injury.
(holding a light over Roderigo): Do we know
this man, or not?
Alas, it is my dear friend Roderigo!
It can't be. Yet it is. Heavens! Roderigo!
(to Cassio): What malice was between you?

CASSIO: None. I don't even know him.

IAGO *(to Bianca):* Why, you look very pale.

The terror in your eyes hints at guilt.
(to the others): Carry them away. I will send
a doctor for Cassio.

*(**Cassio** and **Roderigo** are carried off. Enter **Emilia**.)*

EMILIA: What's the matter, husband?

IAGO: Cassio was attacked here in the dark
By Roderigo and others who escaped.
He was almost killed. Roderigo is dead.

EMILIA: Oh, alas, good Cassio!

IAGO: This is what comes of whoring.
Please, Emilia, go ask Cassio where he
had supper tonight.
(to Bianca): What? Does my question make
you shake?

BIANCA: He had supper at my house—but
I'm not shaking because of that.

IAGO: Oh, he did? I order you, come with me.

EMILIA: Curses on you, harlot!

BIANCA: I am no harlot. I am as honest as
any of my accusers.

EMILIA: Nonsense! Curses on you!

IAGO: Let's get a doctor for Cassio.
(to Bianca): Come along, woman. You'd
better come up with another story.
Emilia, run to the castle

And tell my lord and lady what has
   happened. Hurry!

(They exit.)

| Scene 2 |

*(**Desdemona** is sleeping in a bedchamber in the
castle. Enter **Othello** with a candle.)*

OTHELLO: I'll not shed her blood nor scar
   Her skin, which is whiter than snow.
   Yet she must die, or she'll betray more
     men.
   I'll put out this light, and then put out
     her light. *(He kisses her.)*
   Her sweet breath almost persuades me to
     spare her.
   One more kiss, one more! This is the last!
   Such sweetness was never before so fatal.
   I must weep, but they are cruel tears.
   My sorrow is like God's when he punishes
   His beloved sinners. She's waking up.

DESDEMONA: Who's there? Othello?

OTHELLO: Yes, Desdemona.

DESDEMONA: Will you come to bed, my lord?

OTHELLO: Have you prayed tonight?

DESDEMONA: Yes, my lord.

OTHELLO: Can you think of any sin
That you haven't yet confessed to heaven?
If so, ask forgiveness now.
I don't want to kill your unprepared spirit.

DESDEMONA: What? Do you talk of killing?

OTHELLO: Yes, I do.

DESDEMONA: Then heaven have mercy on me!

OTHELLO: Think about your sins.

DESDEMONA: They are all the different loves
I have for you.

OTHELLO: Yes, and for that you will die.

DESDEMONA: It's unnatural to kill out of love.
What's the matter?

OTHELLO: That handkerchief that I gave
to you—
You gave it to Cassio.

DESDEMONA: No, I swear by my life and soul!
I never wronged you in my life!
I love Cassio only as a friend.
I never gave him a token of love.

OTHELLO: I saw my handkerchief in his hand,
You lying woman!
You have turned my heart into stone.
You make me call what I intend to do
A murder, when I meant it as a sacrifice.
I *saw* the handkerchief!

DESDEMONA: He must have found it, then.
I never gave it to him. Send for him.
Let him confess the truth.

OTHELLO: He has confessed.

DESDEMONA: To what, my lord?

OTHELLO: That he has used you.

DESDEMONA: How? Improperly?

OTHELLO: Yes.

DESDEMONA: He wouldn't say that.

OTHELLO: No, his mouth has been stopped.
I ordered honest Iago to see to it.

DESDEMONA: What—is he dead?

OTHELLO: If all his hairs had been lives, my
revenge would have killed them all.

DESDEMONA: Alas! He has been betrayed,
and I am finished!

OTHELLO: Enough, harlot! Are you weeping
for him to my face?

DESDEMONA: Oh, banish me, my lord, but do
not kill me!

OTHELLO: Down with you, harlot!

DESDEMONA: But let me say one prayer!

OTHELLO: It is too late!

(Othello smothers Desdemona.)

EMILIA *(outside the door)*: My lord, my lord!

OTHELLO *(still smothering Desdemona, as she struggles)*:
What is this noise? Not quite dead?
I may be cruel, but I'm also merciful.
I would not have you linger in your pain.
There, there.

EMILIA *(from offstage)*: My lord, my lord! I need
to talk to you!

OTHELLO *(to Emilia)*: Yes, yes, just a minute!
(to himself): It's Emilia. She's probably come
to tell me of Cassio's death.
(looking at Desdemona): No more movement?
Still as the grave. Shall I let the maid in?
Is that wise?

I think she stirs again. What's best to do?
If the maid comes in, she'll want to speak
  to my wife.
My wife! What wife? I have no wife!
Oh, this is unbearable! Oh, heavy hour!

EMILIA: Let me talk with you, my lord!

OTHELLO: I'll be right there! *(to himself)*: I'll pull
  the curtains closed around the bed.
  (opening the door): What's the matter?

EMILIA: Oh, my good lord, a foul murder has
  been done!
  Cassio has killed a young Venetian named
  Roderigo.

OTHELLO: Roderigo's been killed? And Cassio?

EMILIA: No, Cassio's not been killed.

OTHELLO: Cassio's not been killed? Then the
  wrong murder has been committed
And my sweet revenge has turned bitter.

DESDEMONA *(weakly)*: Wrongly, wrongly
  murdered!

EMILIA: Oh, lord, what is that voice?

OTHELLO: That? What?

EMILIA: Oh, no! That was my lady's voice.
  (pulling back the bed curtains): Help! Help!
  Oh, lady, speak again! Sweet Desdemona!
  Oh, sweet mistress, speak!

DESDEMONA: A guiltless death I die.

EMILIA: Oh, who has done this deed?

DESDEMONA: Nobody. I, myself. Goodbye.
Speak well of me to my kind lord.
Oh, farewell! *(She dies.)*

OTHELLO: It was I who killed her.

EMILIA: Oh, then she's all the more an angel,
And you're an even blacker devil!

OTHELLO: She was unfaithful to me. She was
a whore.

EMILIA: You are slandering her, you devil!
She was as true as heaven!

OTHELLO: Cassio made love to her.
Your husband knew all about it.

EMILIA: My husband?

OTHELLO: Your husband.

EMILIA: That she broke her marriage vows?

OTHELLO: Yes, with Cassio.

EMILIA: My husband!

OTHELLO: Why do you repeat yourself, woman?
I said your husband.
My friend, your husband, honest Iago.

EMILIA: If he said so, may his evil soul
Rot little by little! He's lying.
She was too fond of her filthy marriage.
This deed you've done is no more worthy

of heaven
Than you were worthy of her.

OTHELLO: Ha! You'd better be quiet.

EMILIA: You fool! You dolt! You are
As ignorant as dirt! I'll turn you in
Even if you kill me twenty times.
Help! Help! Somebody, help!
The Moor has killed my lady! Murder!

*(Enter **Montano, Gratiano, Iago,** and **others.**)*

MONTANO: What's the matter?

EMILIA: Oh, you've come, too, Iago?
You've done well, to have other men
Blame their murders on you.
Prove this villain wrong—if you're a man.
He says you told him his wife was false.
I know you didn't. You are not that evil.
Speak, for my heart is in anguish.

IAGO: I told him what I suspected.
It was what he found to be true.

EMILIA: But did you ever say she was false?

IAGO: I did.

EMILIA: You told a lie, a foul, damned lie!
She—with Cassio? Did you say Cassio?

IAGO: With Cassio, woman. Calm down.

EMILIA: I will not calm down. I must speak!
My lady lies here, murdered in her bed—

ALL: Oh, heaven forbid!

EMILIA: And your words, Iago, have brought about this murder.

OTHELLO: Stop staring, gentlemen. It is true.

GRATIANO: This is terrible!

MONTANO: A monstrous act!

EMILIA: Villainy, villainy, villainy!
 I'll kill myself out of grief!

IAGO: Are you mad? I order you to go home.

EMILIA: Perhaps, Iago, I will never go home.

OTHELLO: Oh! Oh! Oh! *(He falls on the bed.)*

EMILIA: Go right ahead and lie there roaring!
 For you have killed the sweetest innocent
 That ever lived.

OTHELLO *(rising)*: Oh, she was wicked!
 It's a pity, but still, Iago knows that
 She and Cassio committed the act of
  shame a thousand times.
 And she rewarded these foul acts
 With a pledge of love that I first gave her.
 I saw the handkerchief in his hand—
 An old gift my father gave my mother.

EMILIA: Oh, God! Oh, heavenly God!

IAGO: By God, keep quiet!

EMILIA: I'll speak as freely as the north wind.
 Oh, you stupid Moor! That handkerchief
 I found only by chance and gave it to

my husband,
For often, with solemn earnestness
He begged me to steal it.

IAGO: You villainous whore!

EMILIA: Did she give it to Cassio? No.
I found it—and I gave it to my husband.

IAGO: You filthy thing, you lie!

EMILIA: By heaven, I do not, gentlemen.
(to Othello): You murderous idiot!
Why did such a fool have so good a wife?

(Othello attacks Iago but is stopped by Montano. Iago stabs Emilia with his sword.)

GRATIANO: He has killed his wife.

EMILIA: Yes, yes. Lay me by my lady's side.

*(Exit **Iago**.)*

GRATIANO: He's gone, but his wife is killed.

MONTANO: What a villain! Use this weapon
Which I have just taken from the Moor
To guard the outside door. Kill him if
He tries to leave. I'll go after Iago,
For he is a damned scoundrel.

*(Exit **Montano** and **Gratiano**, leaving **Othello** and **Emilia** alone.)*

OTHELLO: I seem to have lost my courage.
Now any weakling can take my sword!

But why should my honor outlive me?
Let me lose everything.

EMILIA: Moor, she was chaste.
She loved you, cruel Moor.
I speak the truth—and I die. *(She dies.)*

OTHELLO: I have another sword in this room.
Oh, here it is. *(calling outside)*: Uncle, I
must come out!

GRATIANO *(from offstage)*: If you try it, it will
cost you dearly.
You have no weapon, and would lose.

OTHELLO: Come in, then, and speak with me,
Or I'll attack, even though I'm unarmed.

*(Enter **Gratiano**.)*

GRATIANO: What is the matter?

OTHELLO: Look, I *do* have a weapon.
Don't be afraid. This is my journey's end.
(to Desdemona): How do you look now?
Oh, ill-fated woman! Pale as your gown!
Cold, cold, my girl! Just like your virtue.
Oh, what a cursed fool I am!
Whip me, you devils.
Take this heavenly sight from my mind!
Wash me in gulfs of liquid fire!
O Desdemona! Dead, Desdemona! Dead!
Oh! Oh! Oh!

*(Enter **Lodovico**, **Montano**, **Cassio** carried in a chair, and **Officer**, with **Iago** as a prisoner.)*

LODOVICO: Where is this unfortunate man?

OTHELLO: He who was once Othello? Here.
(to Iago): You *devil! (He stabs Iago.)*

LODOVICO: Get the sword away from him!

(Othello is disarmed.)

IAGO: I'm bleeding, sir, but not killed.

OTHELLO: I am not sorry. I'd rather you live,
For, to my mind, it's happiness to die.

LODOVICO: Did you and he plot to kill Cassio?

OTHELLO: Yes.

CASSIO: Dear General, I gave you no cause.

OTHELLO: I believe you, and I ask your pardon!
Ask Iago why he trapped me into this.

IAGO: Ask me nothing. I won't speak again.

OTHELLO *(to Iago):* You hateful coward.
Cassio, how did you get that handkerchief
That was my wife's?

CASSIO: I found it in my room. Iago confessed
That he left it there on purpose
In order to carry out his plan.

OTHELLO: Oh, I am a fool! A fool! A fool!

CASSIO: We found a letter written by
Roderigo.

He accuses Iago of making him
Bait me when I was on watch,
Which led to my dismissal.
So even now he speaks,
Long after his death.
Iago ruined him.
Iago led him on.

LODOVICO *(to Othello)*: Come with us.
Your power and your command are taken.
Cassio now rules in Cyprus. As for Iago—
If any torture can torment him greatly,
It shall be used against him.
You shall be kept a close prisoner
Until the nature of your crimes is known
To the Venetian state. Come, let's go.

OTHELLO: Wait! A word or two before you go.
I beg you, when you tell of this, speak
Of one that loved not wisely but too well.
Of one not easily jealous, but being
Disturbed, grew extremely confused.
Of one whose hand threw a pearl away
Worth more than all his people.
Write all this! Also say that once,
When a vicious Turk in a turban
Attacked a Venetian and insulted the state,
I took the dog by the throat
And killed him—like this. *(Stabs himself with a knife he had hidden.)*

LODOVICO: Oh, what a bloody end!

OTHELLO *(to Desdemona)*: I kissed you before I
  killed you.
  Now there is no way but this,
  Killing myself, to die with a kiss.

(Falls on the bed, kisses her, and dies.)

LODOVICO *(to Iago)*: Oh, Spartan dog!
  Look at the tragic victims on this bed.
  This is your work. The sight is horrible.
  Let it be hidden.
  (to Gratiano): Gratiano, guard the house
  And take the Moor's property,
  Since you are the heir.
  (to Cassio): Lord Governor, it is your duty
  To see that this hellish villain is punished.
  I'll leave at once and, with a heavy heart,
    report to the state
  These sad acts.

*(**All** exit.)*